Jun. 10, 2009

HOT IRON

The Adventures of a Civil War Powder Boy

by Michael Burgan
illustrated by
Pedro Rodríquez

J
BUR

Librarian Reviewer
Laurie K. Holland
Media Specialist (National Board Certified), Edina, MN
MA in Elementary Education, Minnesota State University, Mankato

Reading Consultant
Elizabeth Stedem
Educator/Consultant, Colorado Springs, CO
MA in Elementary Education, University of Denver, CO

Graphic Flashbacks are published by Stone Arch Books,
151 Good Counsel Drive, P.O. Box 669,
Mankato, Minnesota 56002.
www.stonearchbooks.com

Library of Congress Cataloging-in-Publication Data
Burgan, Michael.
    Hot Iron: The Adventures of a Civil War Powder Boy / by Michael Burgan;
illustrated by Pedro Rodríquez.
        p. cm. — (Graphic Flash)
        ISBN-13: 978-1-59889-311-3 (library binding)
        ISBN-10: 1-59889-311-4 (library binding)
        ISBN-13: 978-1-59889-406-6 (paperback)
        ISBN-10: 1-59889-406-4 (paperback)
        1. Graphic novels. I. Rodríquez, Pedro. II. Title.
PN6727.B855H67 2007
741.5'973—dc22   2006028032

Summary: Twelve-year-old Charlie O'Leary signs aboard the USS Varuna as it steams its
way toward the mouth of the Mississippi River to fight the Confederate Navy. Charlie is
short enough, and swift enough, to race through the crowded ship and fetch gunpowder
for the big guns on deck. The cannons boom like thunder. Their hot iron shells blast
through enemy ships, ripping canvas, wood, and metal. Charlie hopes to find his brother
Johnny among the Varuna's fleet. But will their ships survive the awesome Battle of New
Orleans?

Art Director: Heather Kindseth
Graphic Designer: Brann Garvey

1 2 3 4 5 6 11 10 09 08 07 06

Printed in the United States of America.

TABLE OF CONTENTS

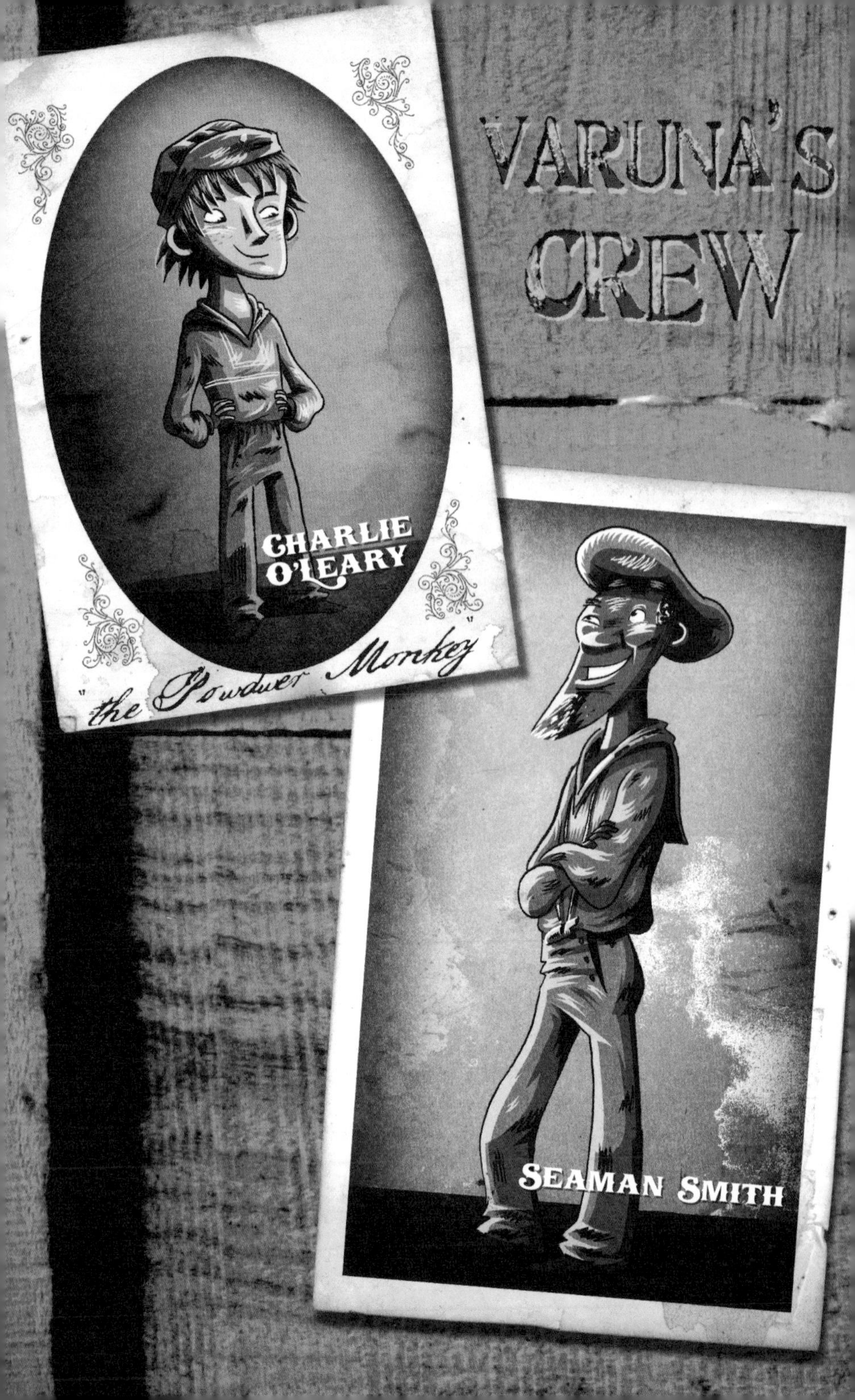
VARUNA'S CREW
CHARLIE O'LEARY
the Powder Monkey
SEAMAN SMITH

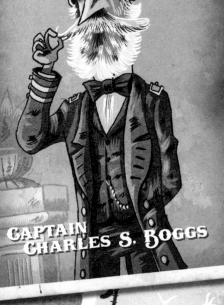

**CAPTAIN
CHARLES S. BOGGS**

**SEAMAN
THOMAS
BOURNE**

**OTHER
SAILORS ON THE VARUNA**

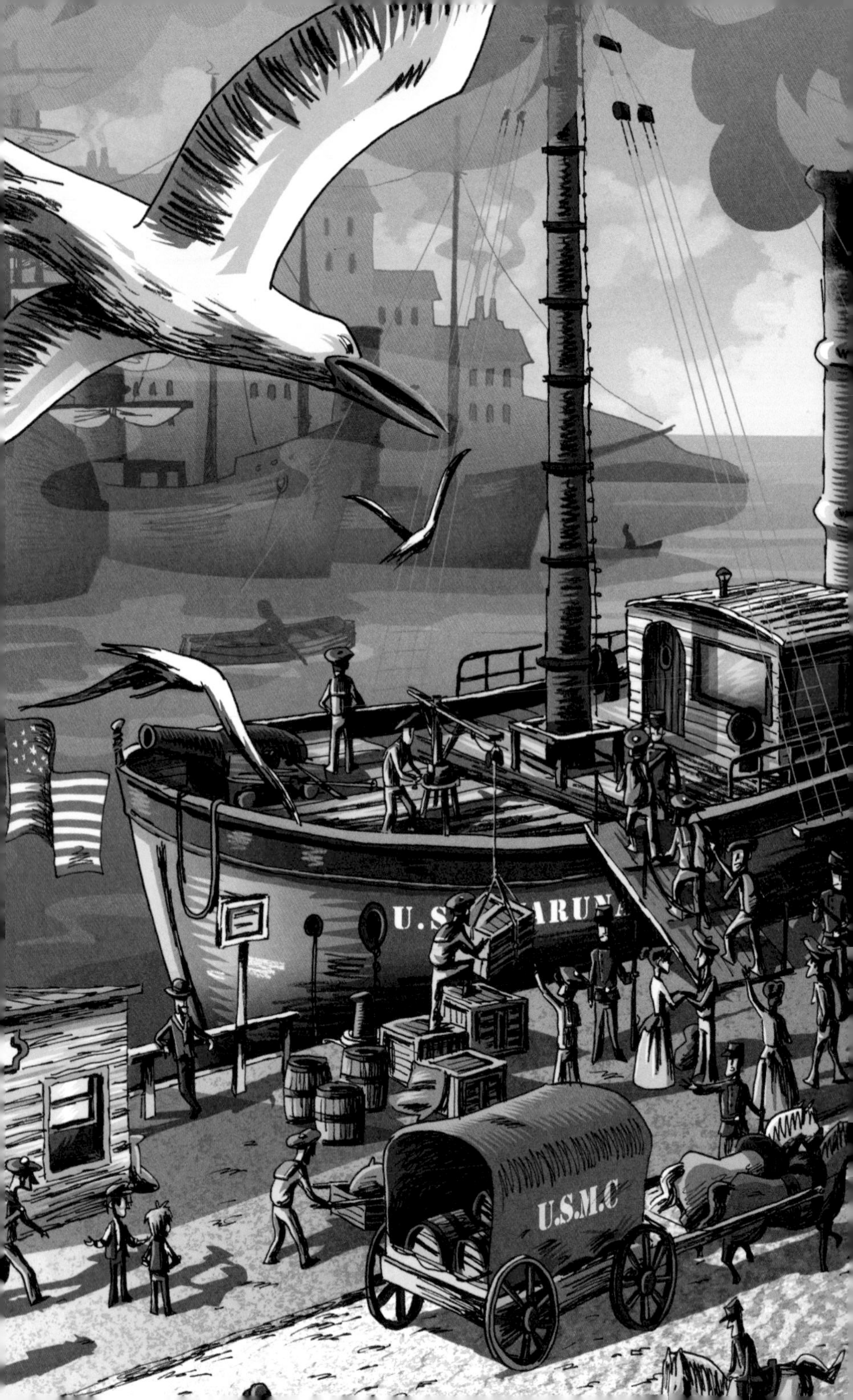
U.S.M.C

★ Chapter One ★
JOINING THE FIGHT

Charlie O'Leary knew his time had come. Now that he was 12, he was ready to go off to sea. The Civil War had been raging for almost a year, and the North needed sailors for its battle against the South.

A cold February wind blew through the bustling streets of New York City as Charlie and his friend Amos reached the docks.

"You're crazy, Charlie," said Amos. "The Union Navy won't take you. You're too young, and too small."

"I'm not leaving this dock until some captain takes me on," said Charlie.

"Which ship will you try?" asked Amos.

Charlie's eyes were drawn to the *Varuna*, a new Navy ship boasting ten cannons. Without a word, Charlie boldly boarded her. A few sailors watched him march ahead.

"Get a load of this little guy," one sailor said.

"Must be one of the new officers," another one joked.

Finally, Charlie found his way to Charles S. Boggs, captain of the *Varuna*. This was it, Charlie thought. He took a deep breath as he approached the man towering above him.

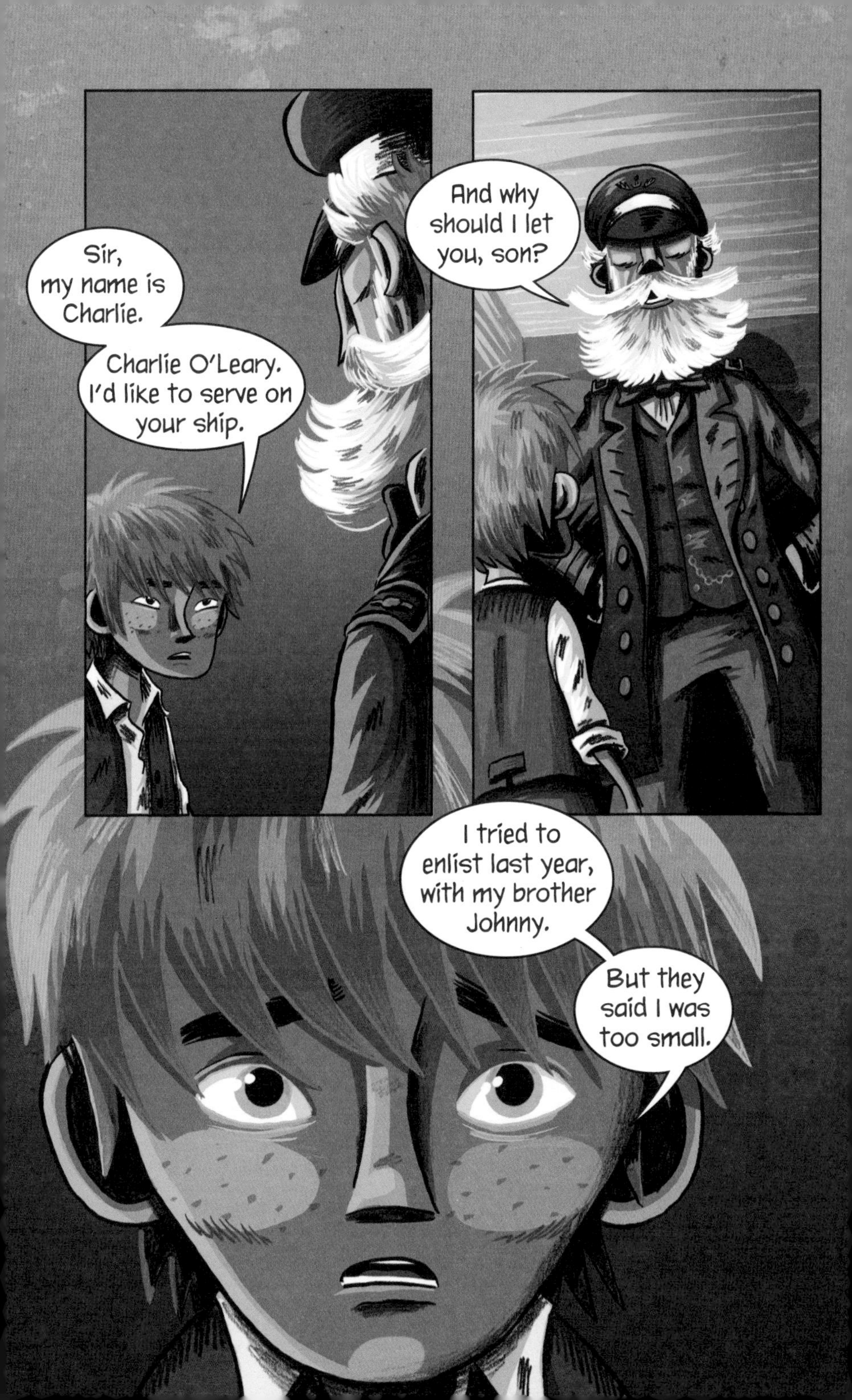
Sir,
my name is
Charlie.
Charlie O'Leary.
I'd like to serve on
your ship.
And why
should I let
you, son?
I tried to
enlist last year,
with my brother
Johnny.
But they
said I was
too small.

Captain Boggs studied Charlie. "You want to help the Union, just like your brother?" he said.

"Yes, sir," Charlie replied. "I promised Johnny I'd get to sea and fight alongside him."

Charlie tried not to show how much he was shaking. Sailors can't be nervous, he thought.

"The Navy was right the first time," said Boggs. "You are small."

Charlie's heart sank.

"But that might be just what I need," said Boggs.

Charlie watched as a sailor sprinted from one of the *Varuna's* guns to where the captain stood.

"Boys his age have been at sea forever," said Boggs. "And he wants to fight."

"Yes, sir," said Bourne.

"Make the boy a Third Class — no, a Second Class Boy," said Boggs. "The pay is $8 a month, Charlie."

"Money doesn't matter," said Charlie. "I'd do it for free, sir."

Boggs put his hand on Charlie's shoulder.

"Good attitude, boy," said Boggs. "Let's see if it rubs off on the men on this ship."

Boggs smiled and then walked down the deck.

Bourne put his hands on his hips. "Lucky you," he said to Charlie. "First day and you already got a promotion. Well, c'mon, boy, follow me."

The ship buzzed with activity as the men prepared to sail. The *Varuna* held about 80 sailors, Charlie guessed. A good many were black men. Even though Charlie had grown up in the gigantic city of New York and seen many kinds of people, he had never seen blacks and whites working together before.

He followed Bourne across the ship and then down below the main deck.

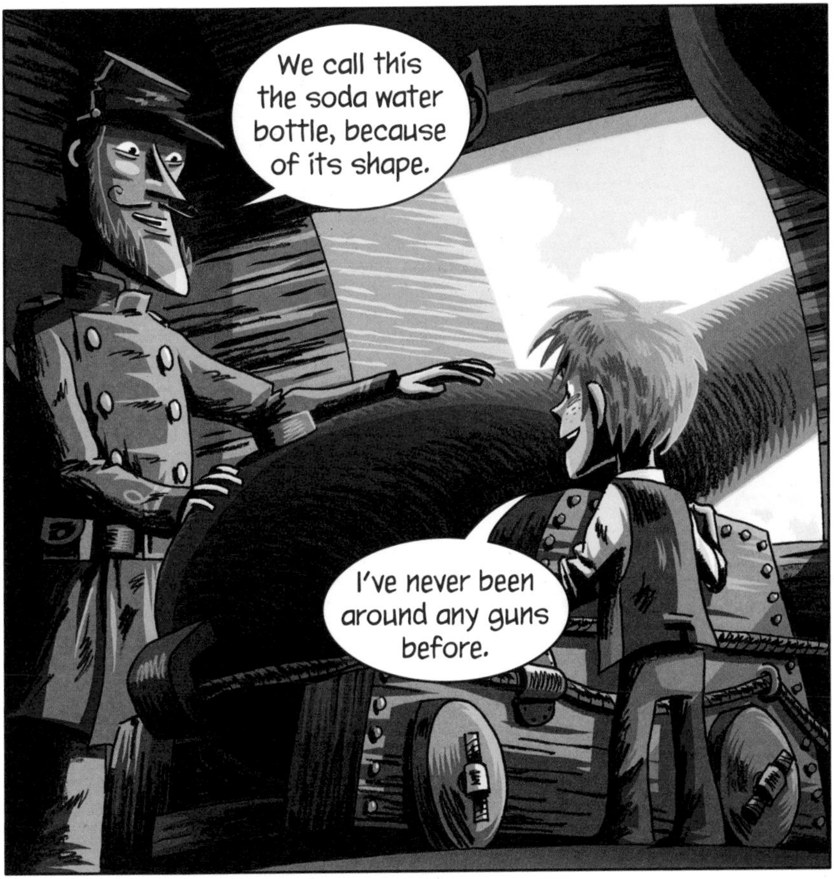
We call this the soda water bottle, because of its shape.
I've never been around any guns before.

Several sailors now approached the gun. They eyed Charlie with suspicion.

"What's this?" one of them asked. "Are we giving tours now to landlubbers?"

"Smith," Bourne said, "this is your new powder monkey."

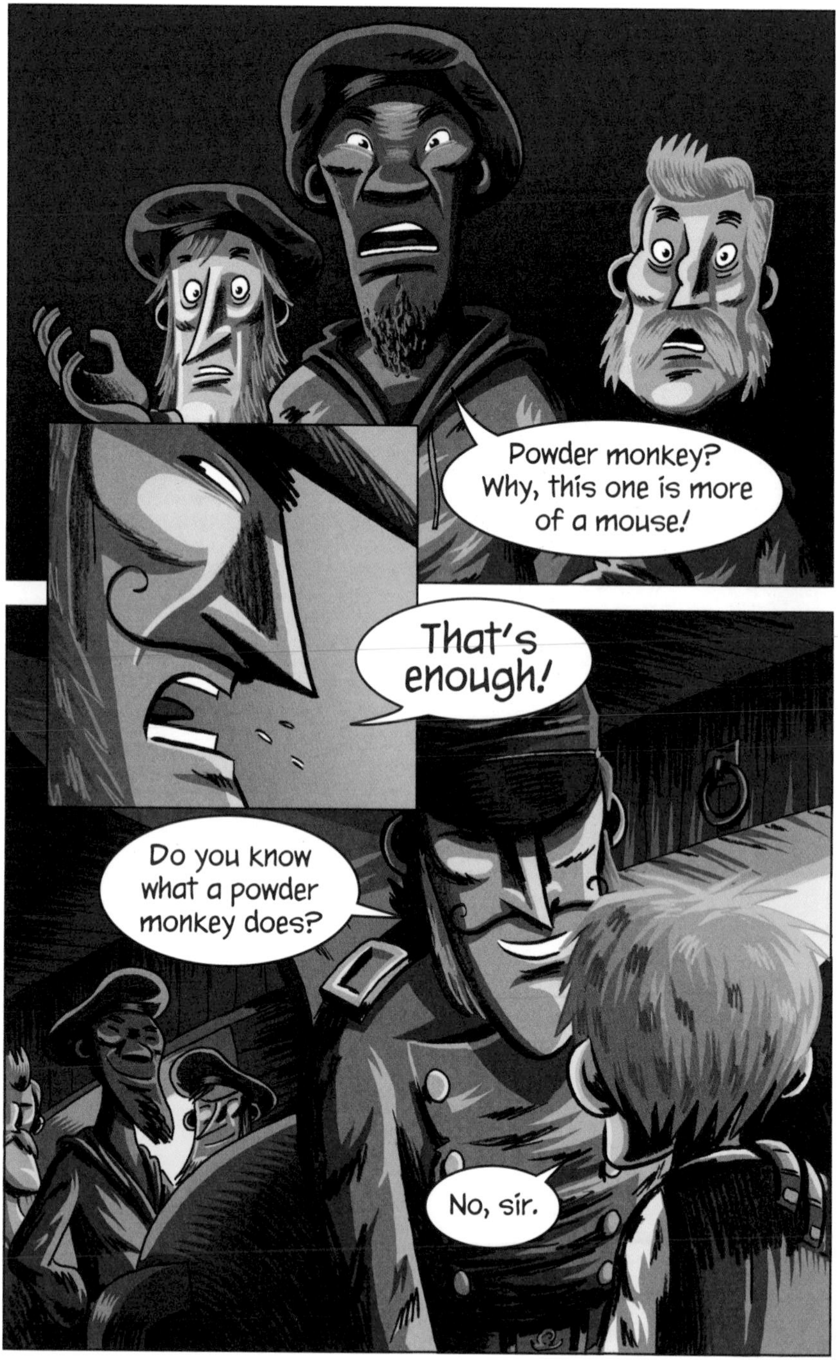
Powder monkey? Why, this one is more of a mouse!
That's enough!
Do you know what a powder monkey does?
No, sir.

Bourne explained that the boys called powder monkeys had to make sure their gun crews always had gunpowder.

The powder came in small packets called charges. The charges were kept in a special room called the magazine. The powder boys had to run down to the magazine, grab a charge, and then run back up to the gun crew. When the powder was poured into the cannon and lit, it exploded, firing out the shell inside the gun.

Short boys were perfect for running through the narrow passages and low rooms of the ship. And a fast boy, who ran as quick as a monkey, was the best helper a gun crew could have.

"Can you do it, Charlie?" Bourne asked.

"Aye, aye, sir!" said Charlie.

Smith whispered to himself, "So now our lives depend on the little mouse."

★ Chapter Two ★
PREPARING FOR BATTLE

The next day, the *Varuna* sailed. Black smoke poured from the ship's stack as the steam engine clanged below deck. Seeing the other sailors at work, Charlie wondered what his brother Johnny was doing out on his ship.

Charlie stood by the gunwale, the side of the ship, and stared out at the endless ocean.

A loud voice interrupted his thoughts. "Come on, Mouse! This is no pleasure cruise!"

It was Smith, standing behind Charlie.

"You've got work to do," added Smith.

Charlie soon learned that running and getting powder was just one of his many jobs.

In the days to come, Charlie cleaned more than he ever had in his life. There was brass to polish and decks to wash. But finally, Bourne and his gun crew practiced their main job.

Faster, Charlie! We need that powder.

On his second run from the magazine . . .

Ahhhh!

All morning, Charlie ran back and forth
between the decks, bringing powder to the gun
crew. A few more times he dropped the charges,
or tangled himself up in the legs of the busy
sailors rushing around the ship. Finally, the
practice ended.

Charlie found a corner of the deck where he
could sit alone and think about his day. He was
glad his brother Johnny wasn't there to see how
badly his practice had gone.

"Hey, Mouse!" yelled a sailor. "Captain wants to see you."

Great, Charlie told himself. I'll probably get tossed overboard. Or locked away in the brig.

Charlie knocked on the door to the captain's quarters and was told to enter. He saw Captain Boggs sitting behind a huge table that was covered with maps. A second officer, one Charlie didn't recognize, stood nearby. The second officer didn't look much older than Johnny.

"I heard you had a rough day today, Second Class Boy O'Leary," said Boggs.

Charlie nodded.

"Your gun crew relies on you, Charlie," Boggs said. "You have to do better."

"I will, sir," said Charlie. "I promise."

"Then carry on, O'Leary," said Boggs.

In the weeks to come, Charlie practiced hard. He also learned to hand out the charges from the magazine. The men who worked inside the magazine kept the charges behind wet curtains. Dry powder was so quick to burn, that the wet curtains prevented any powder from exploding by mistake.

The days seemed to last forever, and Charlie sometimes caught himself nodding off to sleep. But he always snapped up and began working again, harder than before.

The *Varuna* was steaming south, toward the Gulf of Mexico, to join a fleet under the command of David Farragut. The fleet's target was the city of New Orleans, the major Rebel port on the Mississippi River. Taking New Orleans was the first step in the Union's plan to control the important river.

One April morning, Charlie rolled out of his hammock and looked out across the water.

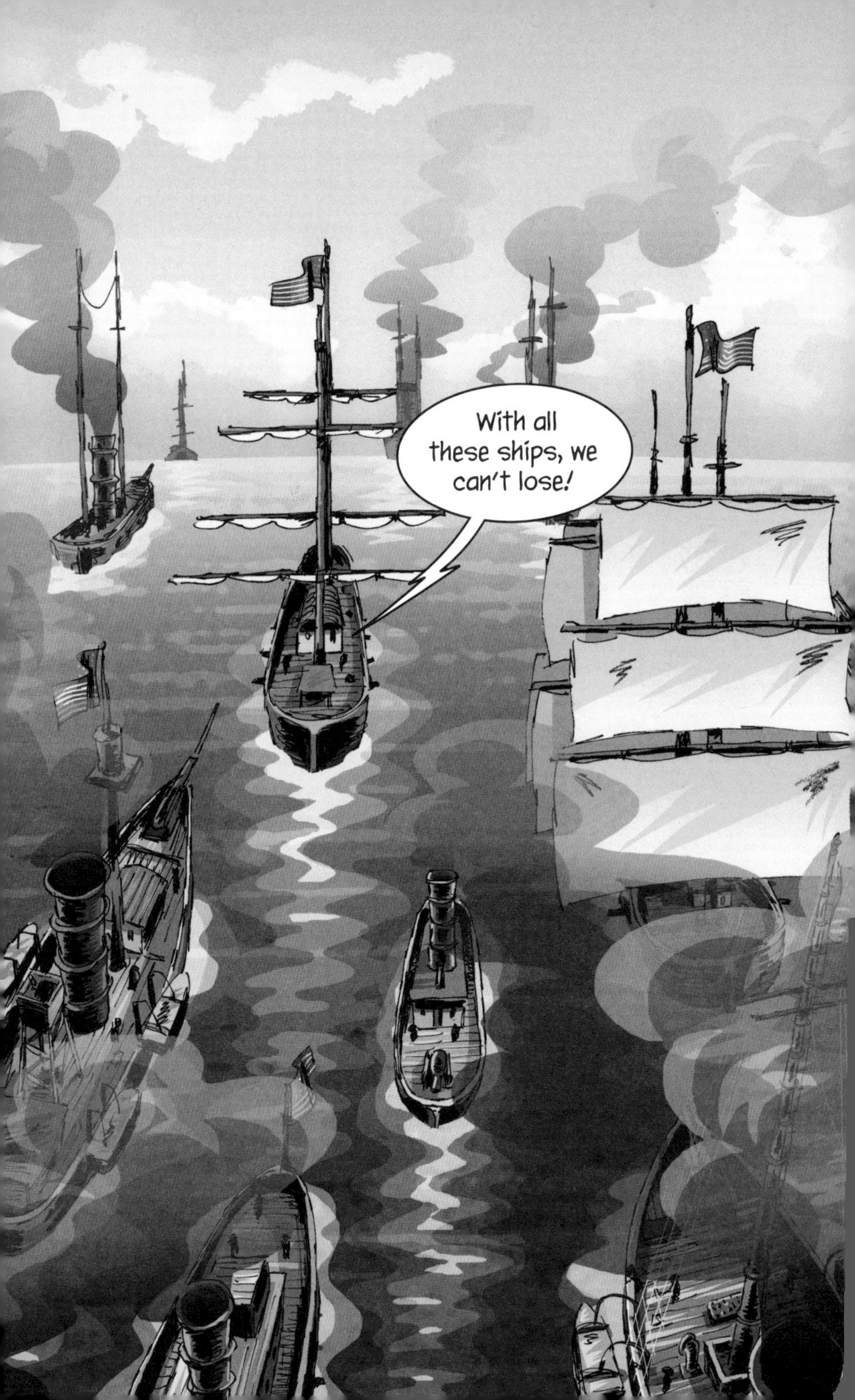
With all these ships, we can't lose!

Charlie's thoughts turned to Johnny again. His brother could be on one of those Union ships, preparing for battle. How could he find out? Finally, Charlie asked Bourne to help him look for his brother.

Later that day, another response came from the *Cayuga* crew: "A sailor by the name of O'Leary is on the *Pensacola*."

"That must be him!" thought Charlie.

For the next two days, the crew prepared the *Varuna* for battle. Fighting could begin at any time. Before the ship reached New Orleans, she had to steam past two Confederate posts that guarded the route, Forts Jackson and St. Philip.

The Union ships slowly sailed up the waterway and entered the mouth of the great Mississippi River.

Charlie watched the *Pensacola*, just three ships ahead of the *Varuna*. As the ships rounded a bend, Charlie could see the two forts. The Confederate flags waved boldly above them.

Flag Officer Farragut had sent mortar ships ahead. They shot heavy mortar shells into the forts, but the Rebels kept fighting. After two days of constant shelling, Charlie thought he would go deaf from all the booming and crashing.

Finally, on April 24, the order came. The Union ships must pass the forts and attack the city of New Orleans.

In the dark hours of the morning, the *Varuna* and the rest of the fleet steamed silently upriver.

When the moon rose, however, the ships were plain to see in the bright silver light. Charlie watched as Rebel cannon balls and shells flew toward the sails of the Union ships.

The Confederate ship *Governor Moore* had slipped through the smoke of the Union mortar fire. At the same time, the speedy *Varuna* had sailed past the other Union ships. Now, only the *Moore* could stop it from reaching New Orleans.

For Charlie, the Civil War had finally begun.

★ Chapter Three ★
DIRECT HIT

Charlie lost count of how many times he
ran between the magazine and the cannon that
morning. But he didn't fall. He made sure his
gun crew always had the powder they needed
as they fired at the *Governor Moore*. In the face
of the *Varuna*'s powerful guns, and the booming
from the "soda water bottles," the Rebel ship kept
chasing them up the river.

A sailor ran over to Charlie's crew.

"Hold off, Bourne," he said. "The captain
wants to come around to get a better angle."

As the ship began to turn on the water,
Charlie used the break in the fighting to scan the
river for his brother's ship.

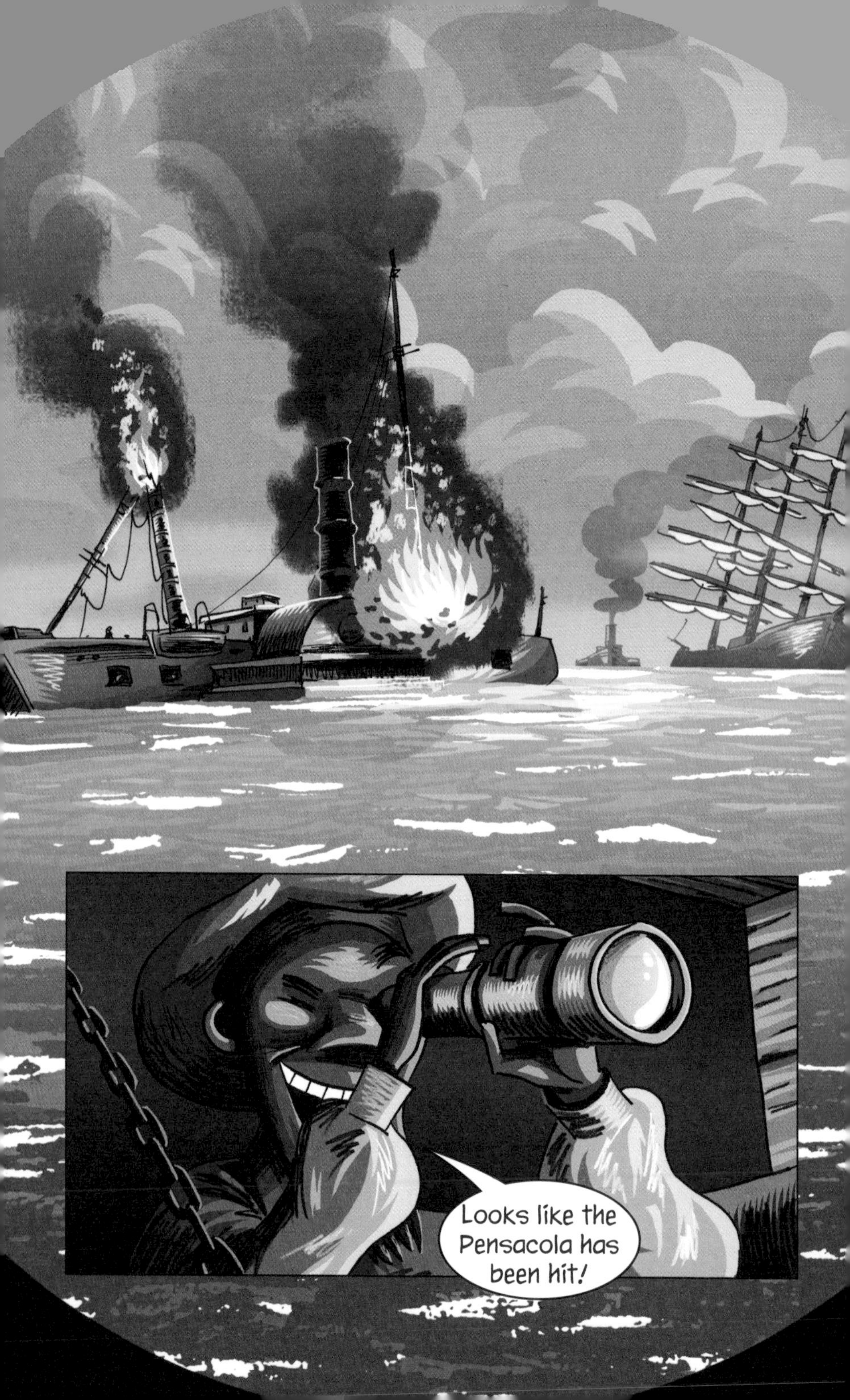
Looks like the Pensacola has been hit!

Where is it? wondered Charlie. It was hard to see through all the cannon smoke floating above the river. It blinded him in the morning sunlight.

"Come on!" shouted Bourne. "We're almost in position. Battle stations!"

Charlie took his place behind the big gun. He could feel the heat from the cannon's iron. He knew that if he touched it, he could burn his hand.

The *Governor Moore* was closer than ever. Charlie reached into his powder sack for a charge. His fingers fumbled with it. *Hurry, hurry!* he told himself. He was too busy thinking about Johnny on the wounded *Pensacola*.

The two ships were now alongside each other.

"We can't miss her now!" said Smith.

"And her guns can't miss us either," Bourne yelled back.

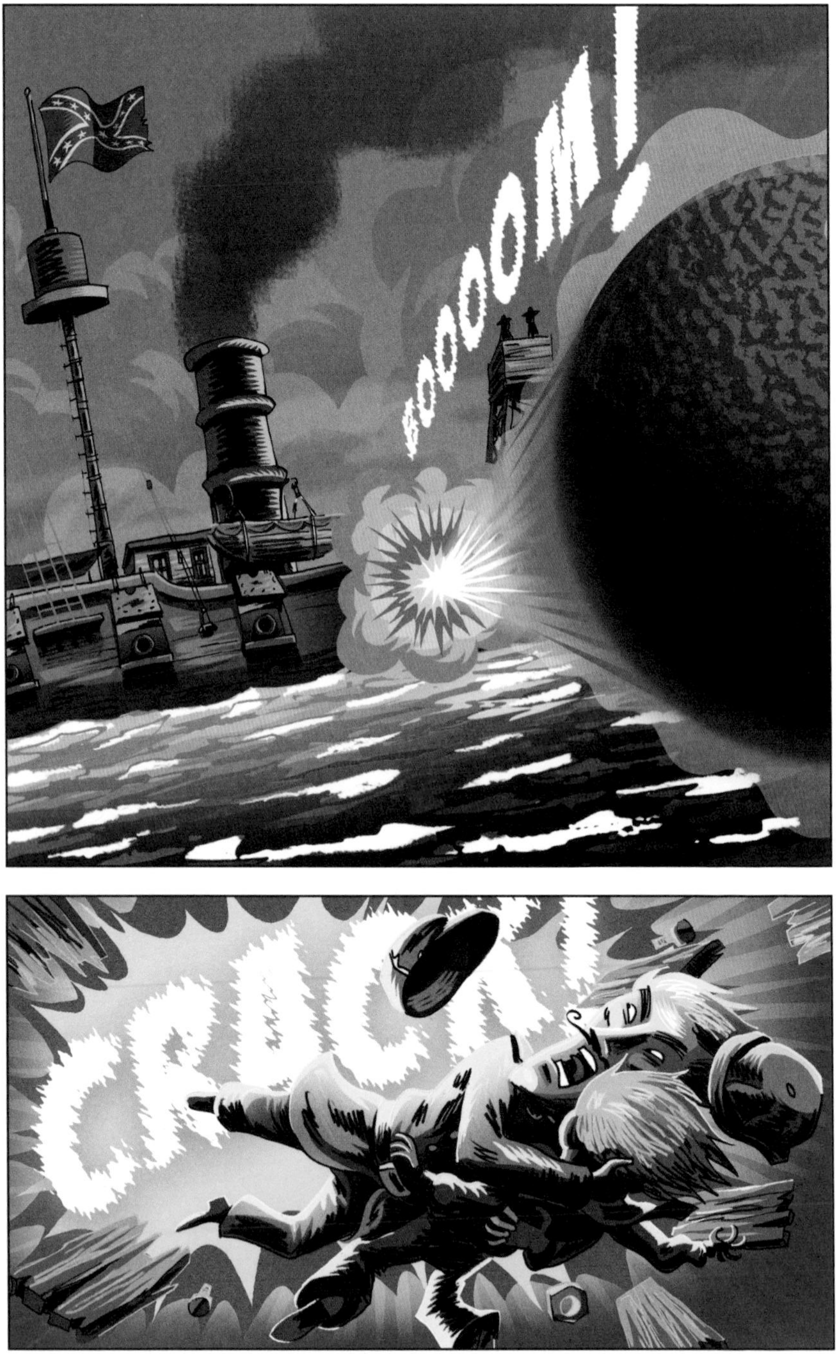
BOOOOM!!
CRAC

The world exploded into a million splinters of wood and canvas. The sky went black. Then, all around him, Charlie heard shouts and groans. The air was full of the smell of blood and gunpowder. Charlie felt his heart pounding, so he knew he was still alive.

But something else was wrong. His legs wouldn't move! Charlie realized something heavy was laying across him. Bourne's body had pinned him to the deck.

"Seaman Bourne, are you all right?" shouted Charlie.

"He's hit," said Smith. "Get him to he doctor."

Two sailors lifted Bourne to his feet.

"No," said Bourne, weakly. "I've got to keep fighting."

"You're crazy, Bourne," said Smith. "Look at your leg. You can't even stand up."

Charlie knew Smith was right. He also saw two dead sailors behind him. Even Smith was bleeding from a wound. Their gun crew, gun number two, was in no shape to keep firing. Unless —

Let me help! I know what to do!

For once, Smith didn't laugh at him. He and the other sailors were silent. All Charlie heard was the boom of the *Moore*'s guns and the shouts of sailors on both ships.

The Mouse might be our only chance.

All right, but I'm staying here.

As the remaining crew scrambled into position, Charlie threw the powder charge into the cannon. Then he shoved it down with the ramrod. After the shell was in the gun, Charlie helped tug on the rope that pulled the cannon into firing position.

"Hurry up and fire that blasted thing!" said Bourne.

Suddenly, Charlie pointed. "Look!" he cried.

Chapter Four

A TASTE OF
HOT IRON

The *Governor Moore's* bow crashed into the
Varuna. The collision was not near Charlie and
his gun crew, but the boy was hurled back as if a
bomb had exploded at his feet.

Charlie had never heard such a terrible noise
before. He knew it was the ripping and tearing of
the *Varuna's* metal plates. It sounded to Charlie
as if the sky itself was breaking apart.

From where he lay on the deck, Smith lifted
up his head. "Anyone hurt?" he cried.

A few men groaned in response. Charlie
struggled to his feet, then dusted himself off.

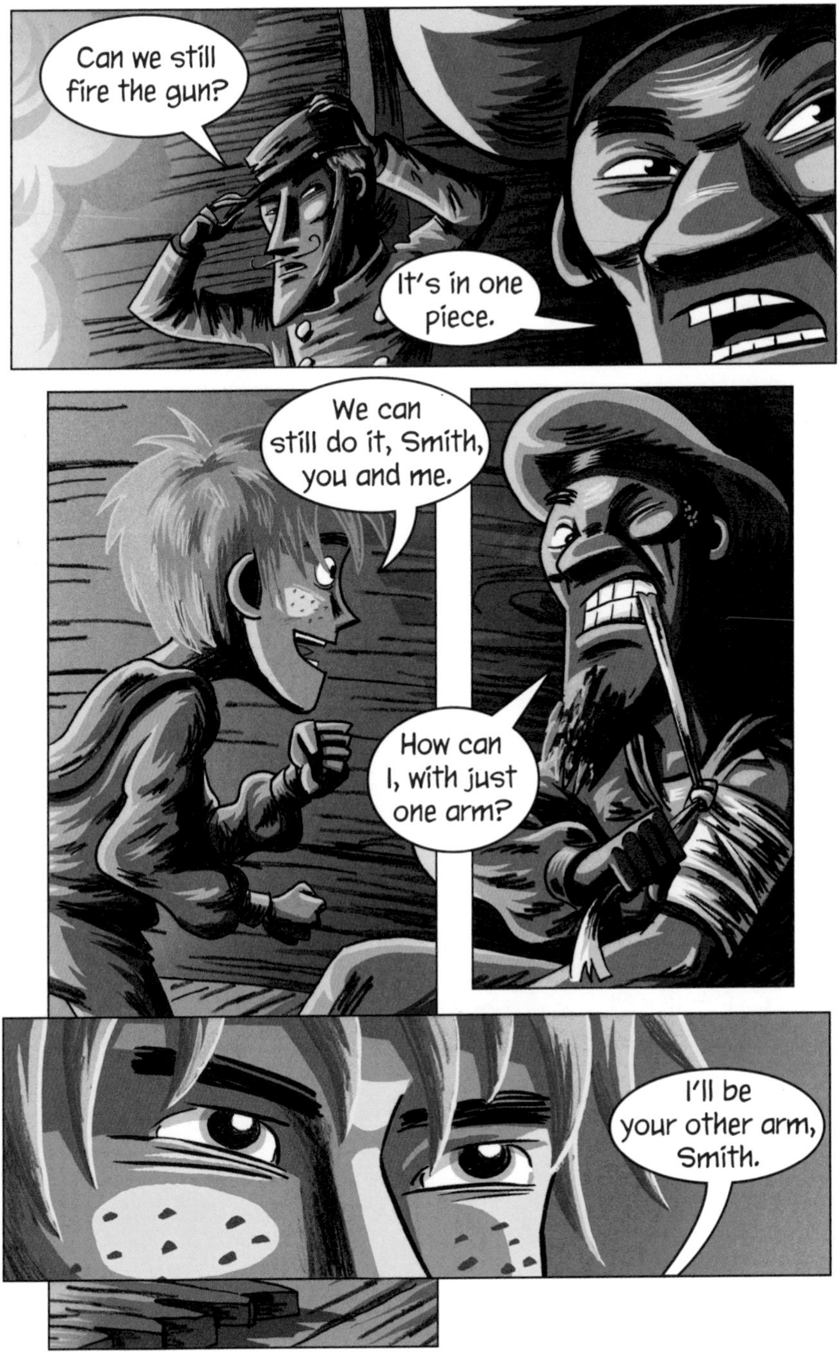
Can we still fire the gun?
It's in one piece.
We can still do it, Smith, you and me.
How can I, with just one arm?
I'll be your other arm, Smith.

Once again, Charlie scrambled to the mouth of the cannon and threw in a charge. Then, Charlie and Smith struggled to load the heavy shell. Finally, Charlie packed everything down with the long ramrod.

Charlie could hear sailors calling for pumps. Water was rushing in where the *Governor Moore* struck them. Charlie blocked out all the noise and confusion. He had his own job to do.

Bourne pushed himself up into a sitting position.

"The captain's bringing us around for another broadside," said Bourne. Charlie braced himself as he felt the ship moving beneath him.

He and Smith strained at the ropes, trying to pull the cannon into the new firing position.

"Can't move it anymore," said Smith. "We have to fire it where it is."

Go ahead, Charlie. Give those Rebs a taste of our hot iron!

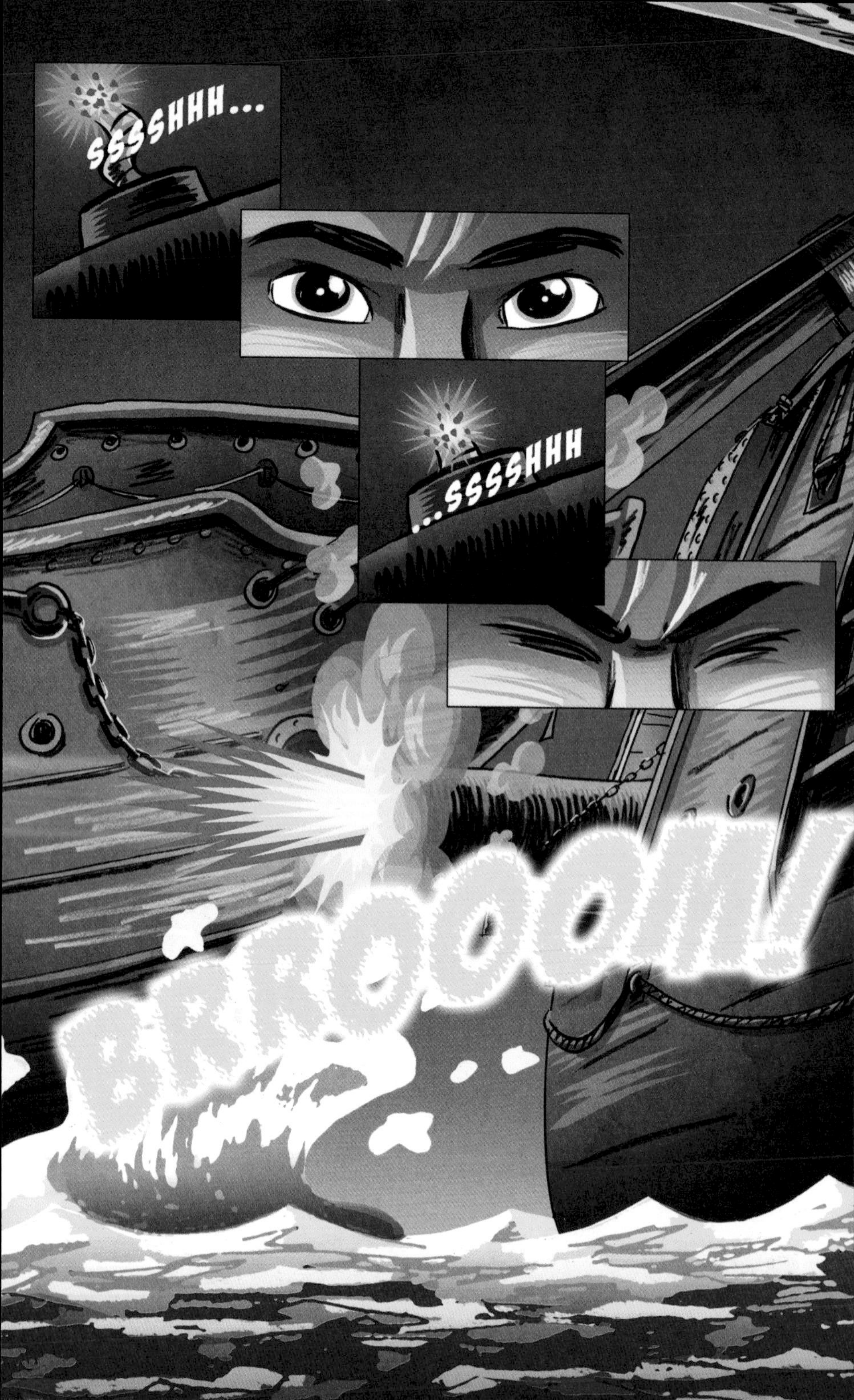
SSSSHHH...
...SSSSHHH
BRROOOM!

Charlie looked through the smoke, trying to watch the shell — his shell — as it raced over the water.

He saw an explosion on the *Governor Moore.* Wood and metal went flying.

Smith grabbed the boy with his good arm. "We did it, Charlie! We got those Rebs!"

"Charlie?" said the boy. "You didn't call me Mouse that time."

Smith beamed at him. "You're not a mouse, or a monkey, lad. You're a real sailor now."

"The battle ain't over, men," said Bourne.

Charlie and Smith prepared to load their gun again. The *Governor Moore* was still sailing, and still deadly. Charlie saw the Rebel ship closing in.

"Here she comes again!" yelled the boy.

"I don't believe it!" shouted Smith.

Whomp!

For a second time, Smith and Charlie were knocked off their feet. Again, Charlie heard the earsplitting wail of the ripping metal and the splintering of the ship's wooden beams.

Charlie felt something sticky on his chin. Blood. My first war wound, he thought.

All at once, Charlie remembered Johnny. What happened to the *Pensacola?* The image of his brother lying on the deck of a sinking ship flashed through his mind.

Charlie crawled over to the railing. He pulled himself up and looked over the side. He could see the faces of the enemy sailors on the nearby *Governor Moore.*

Then he turned and saw something he didn't expect. The shore was getting closer.

The captain's going to beach us, thought Charlie. He doesn't want us to sink out in the deep water.

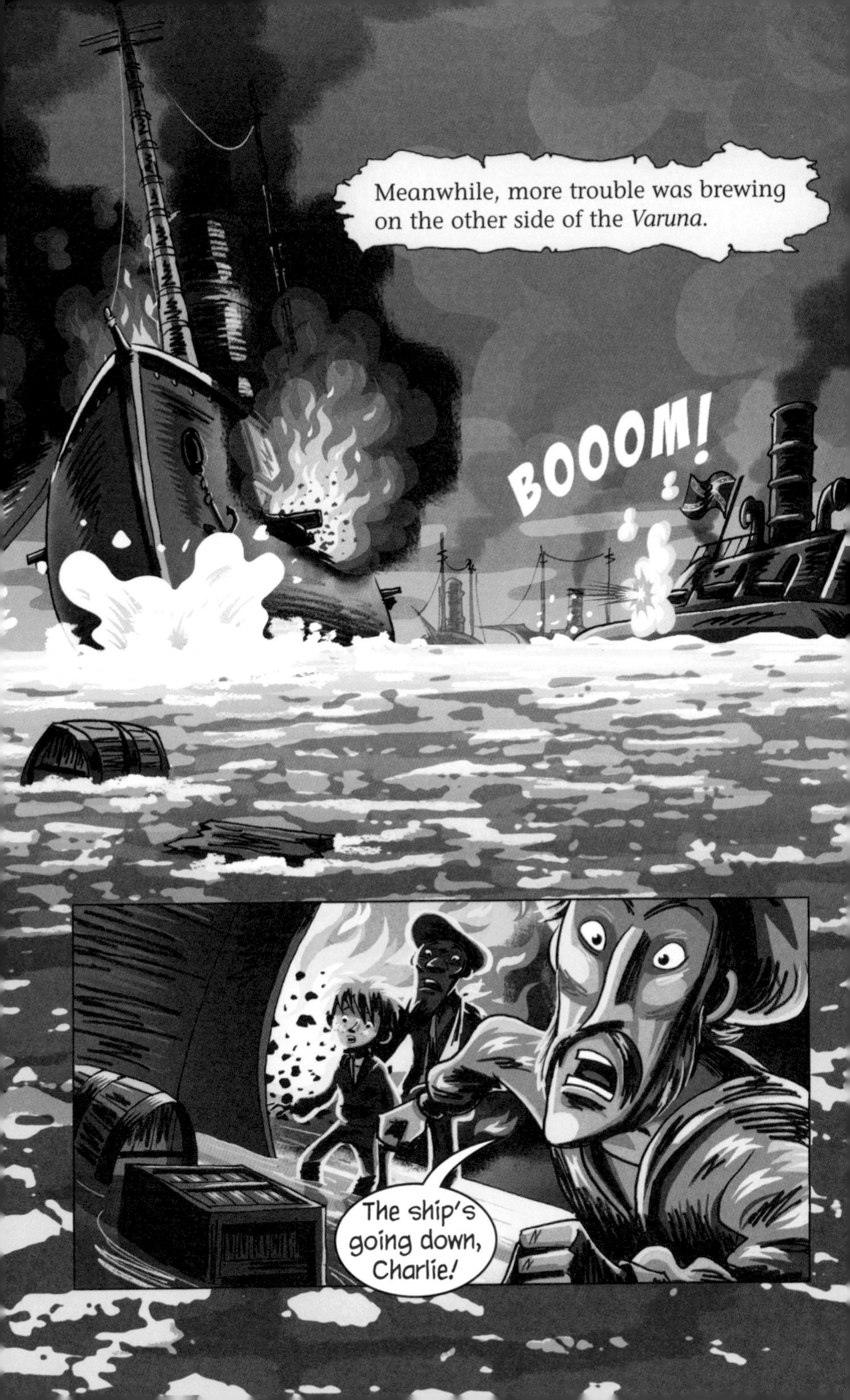
Meanwhile, more trouble was brewing on the other side of the *Varuna*.
BOOOM!
The ship's going down, Charlie!

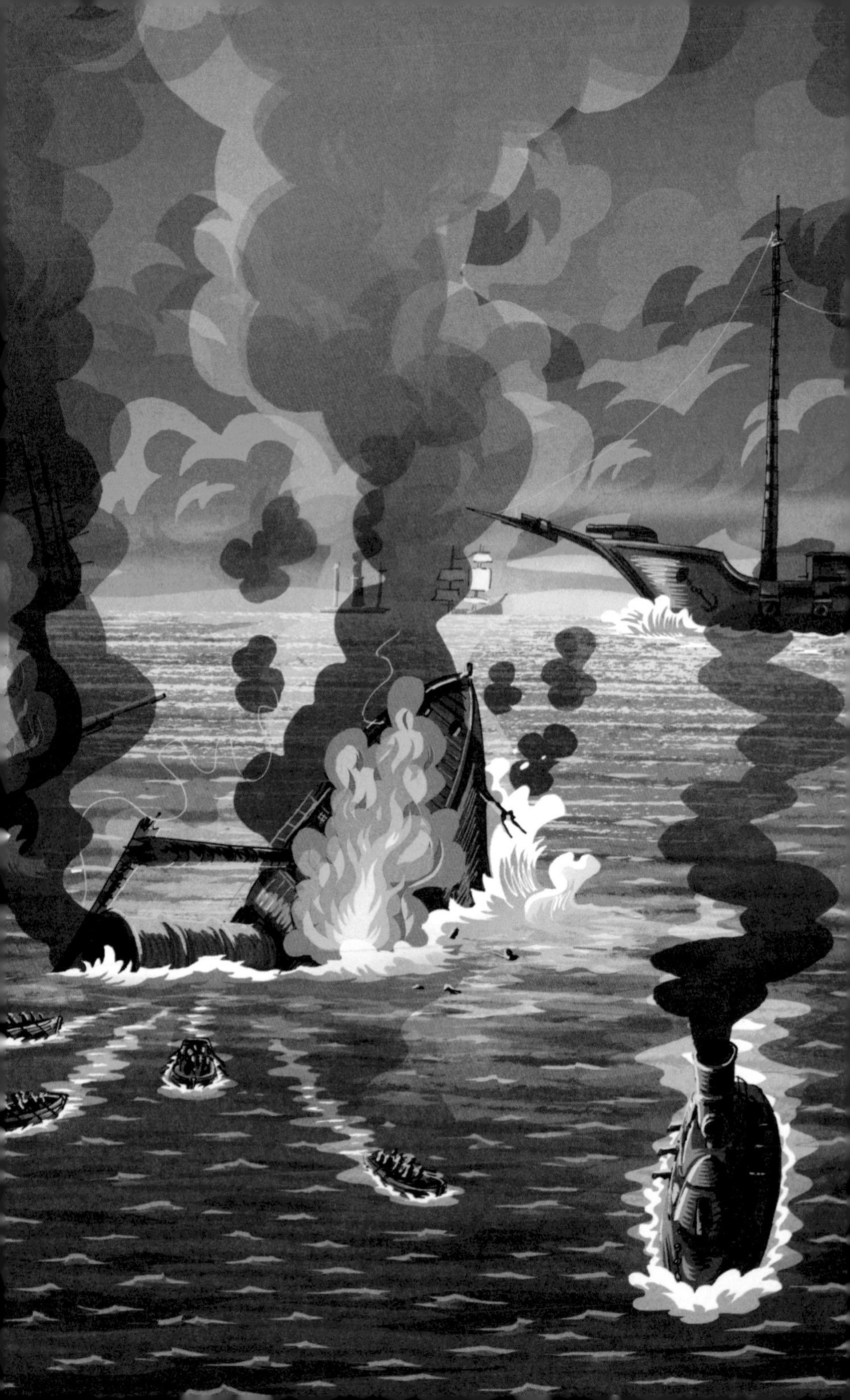

The crew escaped the sinking ship in small rowboats. When they reached the shore, Charlie lay on the beach. His whole body ached. Bourne and Smith dragged themselves off the boat and joined him on the shore. For several minutes, they watched the damaged *Varuna* slowly sink into the mighty Mississippi River.

"Now what do we do?" asked Charlie.

"We wait for one of our ships to pick us up. If the Rebs don't get us first."

"Look!" said Bourne. "Look at the *Moore!*"

The Rebel ship was sinking into the river as well. Smith and Bourne both whooped for joy.

"Ha! We did it!" shouted Bourne. "Look at the smoke pouring out of her! Ha! Our guns did that! Your gun, Charlie!"

But Charlie did not hear Bourne. He lay on the bank of the river in a deep sleep.

Chapter Five

THE FIGHT GOES ON

Charlie didn't sleep long.

Soon one of the ships from the Union fleet came chugging along the river, searching for survivors.

Smith waved at it and a rowboat was sent over to the shore to pick up the members of the *Varuna's* number two gun crew.

Charlie was given a hunk of bread and a cup of coffee. It was delicious. Charlie realized he hadn't eaten since before the battle with the *Governor Moore*.

Then Charlie stood up to stretch his legs. He saw Captain Boggs talking to some of the other *Varuna's* survivors.

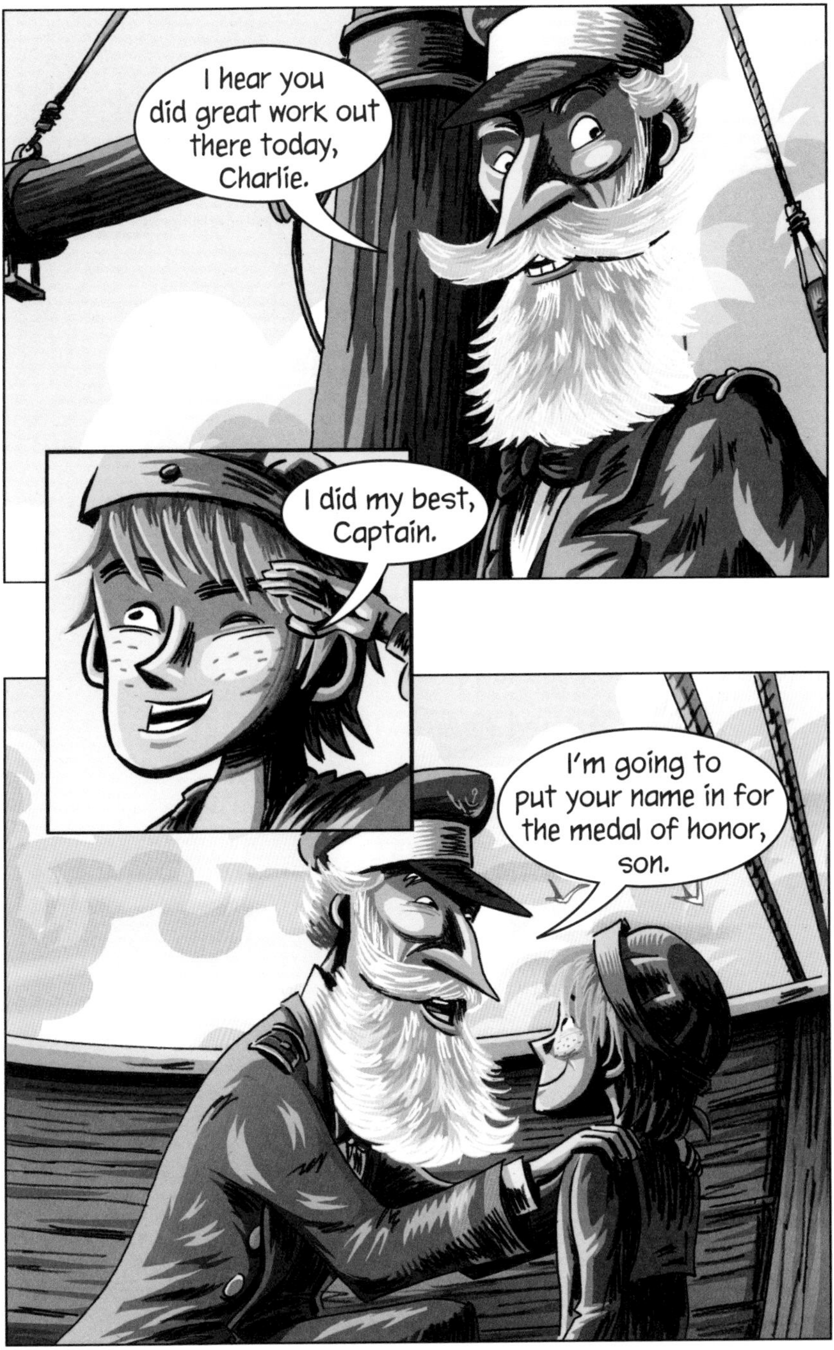
I hear you did great work out there today, Charlie.
I did my best, Captain.
I'm going to put your name in for the medal of honor, son.

Bourne and Smith told the captain more of Charlie's deeds. They told Charlie what an honor it would be for someone his age to win a medal.

The sailors continued to talk, but Charlie now had only one thought on his mind: Johnny.

"Anybody here from the *Pensacola*?" he asked the men sitting and standing on the deck.

The sailors shook their head. Then one man stood up. "I sailed on the *Pensie*," he said.

Charlie rushed over to the man.

"I heard you had a crew member named O'Leary," said Charlie. "I was looking for my brother, Johnny O'Leary."

"How old is your brother?" asked the sailor.

"He's fifteen, sir," said Charlie.

"Our Johnny O'Leary is nearly 40 years old," said the sailor. "He can't be your brother. I'm very sorry."

Charlie walked over to the railing of the ship and watched as they sailed nearer to the city of New Orleans. "He's out there somewhere, Smith," said Charlie. "I can feel it."

"And he's doing what you did," said Smith. "He's fighting for his country, Charlie, and helping his friends."

★ABOUT THE AUTHOR★

Michael Burgan has written more than 90 fiction and non-fiction books for children. A history graduate from the University of Connecticut, Burgan worked at *Weekly Reader* for six years before beginning his freelance career. He has received an award from the Educational Press Association of America and has won several playwriting contests. He lives in Chicago with his wife, Samantha.

★ABOUT THE ILLUSTRATOR★

Pedro Rodríquez studied illustration at the Fine Arts School in Barcelona, Spain. He has worked in design, marketing, and advertising, creating books, logos, animated films, and music videos. Rodríquez lives in Barcelona with his wife, Gemma, and their daughter Maya.

★ GLOSSARY ★

ahoy (uh-HOY)—greeting used by sailors at sea

bow (BOU)—the front of a ship

brig (BRIG)—the jail on board a ship

Confederate (kon-FED-uh-rut)—relating to the Confederate States of America, the Southern states that fought the North in the Civil War

landlubbers (LAND-lub-urz)—people who do not usually sail on a ship

port (PORT)—on a ship, the left side of a ship

ramrod (RAM-rod)—a special pole used to shove items inside a large gun

Rebs, Rebels (REBZ, REB-ulz)—nicknames for the Southern fighters in the Civil War

sharpshooters (SHARP-shute-urz)—soldiers or sailors specially trained to fire rifles at targets from far away

shell (SHEL)—an exploding device fired from a gun

shot (SHAHT)—a solid metal object fired from a gun

starboard (STAR-bord)—on a ship, the right side or something to the right

★ THE ★ CIVIL WAR AT SEA

At the start of the Civil War, the U.S. Navy had only about 40 ships available for service. The government quickly bought merchant ships and turned them into navy ships. It also began building new warships. The Union ship *Varuna* was originally built as a merchant ship.

Seaman Thomas Bourne was an actual sailor on the *Varuna* during the Battle of New Orleans. Bourne was one of eight Union sailors who won the Navy Medal of Honor for his heroics during the battle. Two of the other Medal of Honor winners were teenagers, Third Class Boy George Hollat and Second Class Boy Oscar Peck.

The *Varuna* was named for the Hindu god of the ocean and protecter of the souls of those who drown.

The *Varuna* was one of only four Union ships that did not safely pass the Confederate forts and reach New Orleans. About 40 Union sailors were killed during the fighting.

The Battle of New Orleans made a hero of David Farragut, who commanded the U.S. fleet. Farragut was later named an admiral.

The "soda water bottle" cannons used on the *Varuna* were designed by John Dahlgren. Both the North and the South used his guns, which came in different sizes. The largest weighed more than 20 tons and could fire a shot that weighed 440 pounds.

★ DISCUSSION QUESTIONS ★

1. Charlie was eager to join a ship's crew and fight in the Civil War. Would you want to fight in a war? Why or why not?

2. Do you think Charlie did a good job at being a powder monkey? Do you think young people should be allowed to work with adults in the military?

3. Even during the hardest part of the voyage, when the *Varuna* was being attacked by Confederate gunfire, Charlie never thought of giving up and running away. Why not?

★ WRITING PROMPTS ★

1. Charlie is always thinking of his brother Johnny during his long sea voyage. He even asks sailors on other ships if they have heard of him. Pretend you are on a Civil War ship and want to write a letter to a friend on another ship. What would you say?

2. Look at a map of the United States. Locate New York City and the city of New Orleans. Now draw a map showing the route that Charlie and his shipmates took, and make a list of the states and important cities they would have to pass.

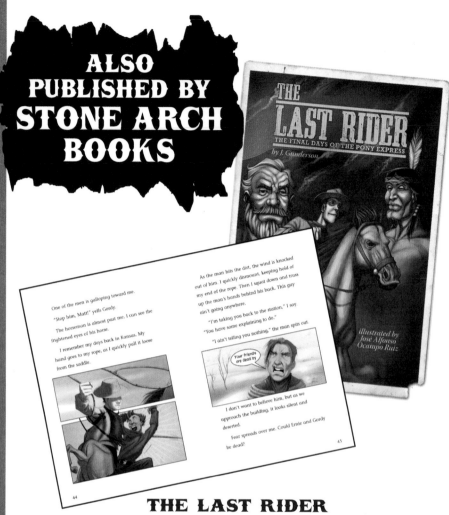

THE LAST RIDER
THE FINAL DAYS OF THE PONY EXPRESS

Matt Edgars hungers for adventure. The Pony Express is the answer to his dreams. Riding fast, riding far, he brings the mail to settlers scattered across the Nevada and Utah deserts. Matt can handle the punishing sun and the poisonous rattlesnakes, but he's worried about rumors of a war with the Paiute nation. Then someone begins setting the Express stations on fire. Are these the last days for the young riders?

BLACKBEARD'S SWORD
THE PIRATE KING OF THE CAROLINAS

Edward Teach, known far and wide as Blackbeard, holds the coast of North and South Carolina in a grip of terror. Lieutenant Maynard and his men of the Royal Navy decide to capture the pirate, but they need help piloting their way through the shallow maze of coves and inlets. They enlist the aid of local fishermen Jacob Webster and his father, but Maynard doesn't count on the fact that Jacob may be leading them into trouble. The boy thinks Blackbeard is a hero!

★ INTERNET SITES ★

Do you want to know more about subjects related to this book? Or are you interested in learning about other topics? Then check out FactHound, a fun, easy way to find Internet sites.

Our investigative staff has already sniffed out great sites for you!

Here's how to use FactHound:

1. Visit *www.facthound.com*

2. Select your grade level.

3. To learn more about subjects related to this book, type in the book's ISBN number: **1598893114**.

4. Click the **Fetch It** button.

FactHound will fetch the best Internet sites for you.